2010

ALL THESE LONELY
PEOPLE

ALL THESE LONELY PEOPLE

Gervase Phinn

BBC
LARGE
PRINT

First published in 2009 by
Penguin Books
This Large Print edition published
2009 by BBC Audiobooks by
arrangement with
Penguin Books Ltd

ISBN 978 1 4056 2260 8

British Library Cataloguing in Publication Data available

Printed and bound in Great Britain by
CPI Antony Rowe, Chippenham and Eastbourne

Chapter One

Father McKenzie could feel pins and needles in his feet. He had been kneeling on the front pew before the altar for a good hour, praying and thinking about what to do. First thing, I suppose, he thought to himself, is to tell the bishop. Then he would break the news to his housekeeper. Thank God there was no wife to tell, no children, no relations.

He lifted his eyes to heaven. The Christ hanging on the huge cross above the altar stared down on him. The eyes were gentle. He didn't look in any pain. There was even a slight smile on the lips, or was he imagining it? The priest noticed more flaking paint on the ceiling, more cracks on the walls, more dust, dirt, decay. There was the damp patch in the shape of a dark monster above the altar in the Lady Chapel. The damp patch brought back a memory.

When he was a young priest he had been sent to a small church in the middle of Ireland. It was in a village in the country, surrounded by pale green hills. There was a little school near the church which he would visit. One morning, when he was talking to the head teacher, a little girl about six years old came up to him. She had long red hair and jade green eyes.

'Hello,' she said.

'Hello,' replied the priest, smiling.

'What is it, Mary?' asked the head teacher sharply.

'It's still there, Miss Martin, in the girls' toilets,' said the girl.

'Is it?' the head teacher replied.

'It is, and it's got bigger.'

'Well, I shouldn't worry about it too much. It won't hurt you.'

'But it's got great curved claws and big jaws and it's turned a mouldy green.'

The head teacher shook her head. 'It can't harm you, Mary.'

'But it puts the fear of God into me every time I look at it,' said the child.

'Well, don't look at it then.'

'Sure, but aren't your eyes just drawn to it?'

'Run along,' said the head teacher crossly. 'It won't hurt you.'

'I can't go to the toilet with it looking down at me, Miss Martin,' said the child.

Father McKenzie asked the child what it was.

'It's a monster,' said the girl, 'a great, dark, green, mouldy old monster with popping eyes and sharp teeth.'

'A monster!' he cried.

'In the girls' toilets.'

'A monster in the girls' toilets?' he repeated.

She patted his arm. 'It's not a real monster,' she said. 'It's a great dark stain from the water leaking through the roof, but it gives me the shivers right enough just to look at it.'

Miss Martin explained that the flat roof always leaked after heavy rain and that the water had left an ugly stain on the wall of the girls' toilets. It had grown in size.

'Is it a very bad leak?' the priest asked.

Before the head teacher could reply, the small girl piped up: 'A bad leak? Sure it'd baptize you!'

He smiled at the memory. Young children were such a delight, so open and honest. Everything in the world for them was new and bright and interesting. Would that it was like that for adults, he thought.

The flaking paint, the cracks, the dust and dirt and the stain would still be there when he was gone, and it would be up to some new priest to try to raise the money to put things right.

*   *   *

Father McKenzie had expected the worst. In his stuffy office, Mr O'Neill, the cancer specialist, had informed him the day before, in the soft but firm voice of a doctor breaking bad news, that the disease had spread. The priest had felt strangely calm.

'How are you feeling, Father?' Mr O'Neill asked.

'A little tired,' the priest replied, 'sometimes I feel sick in the morning, but otherwise I feel fine.'

'Good, good,' the doctor said. He stared down at the notes on his desk. Then he licked a finger and flicked a page. 'It's not good news, I'm afraid.' He didn't look up. 'The lumbar puncture shows that the cancer has spread into your spinal fluid.'

The priest breathed out noisily. 'That bad?'

'I'm afraid so. It's spreading faster than we thought.'

'I suppose the question people ask

at this point is how long?'

'A few months,' the doctor told him, meeting the priest's eyes. 'Maybe a little more. It's always difficult to say. The treatment may help, but—'

'But in my case, it sounds doubtful?'

'I'm afraid so.'

'My father died of cancer, you know,' the priest said. 'Not a day's illness in his life and then he died within the month. Of course he smoked like a chimney. My father was a stubborn man. Even when he was told he had cancer, he carried on smoking. "A bit late in the day to give up," he told me.' The priest paused and gave a small laugh. 'I never smoked.'

'I really am very sorry that the news isn't any better, Father,' the doctor said.

'You have done your best,' the priest told him, getting up to go. 'You couldn't have done any more.

You say I have a few months? Well, at least I'll still be here for Christmas, God willing.'

Father McKenzie sat on the park bench in the bright sunshine before returning to his church. He watched the children in the small playground, running, shouting, laughing, chasing each other. They were so full of life and energy, and he felt suddenly very lonely. He wondered what his child would have looked like if he had married. Would she have had the shiny black hair and dark Irish eyes of his mother? Would he have been like the stocky little boy on the climbing frame, swinging like a monkey on the rope? He said a silent prayer, not to be cured but to have the strength to face what was about to happen to him.

'Good morning.'

Father McKenzie looked up to see the park-keeper. He shielded his eyes from the sun. 'Good morning,' he replied cheerfully.

'Are you here with your grandson?' he was asked.

'No, no,' said the priest. 'I'm just enjoying sitting here watching the children playing and enjoying the sunshine. It's a fine—'

'People might get the wrong idea,' said the park-keeper, his tone of voice suddenly becoming sharp.

'The wrong idea?' repeated the priest.

'Watching the children.'

'I'm not doing any harm,' said the priest. 'As I said, I'm just sitting enjoying the sunshine and watching the little children play. Where's the harm in that?'

'I've seen you here before.'

'I often come here,' the priest told him. 'I enjoy sitting in the park.'

'You always sit on the same bench.'

'That's right.'

'Facing the children's playground.'

'Is there something wrong in that?' asked the priest.

'Well, if I were you, I'd sit

8

somewhere else,' said the park-keeper. 'We've had complaints.'

'Complaints?' said the priest. 'I don't know what you mean.'

'From the mothers, about men such as you watching their kiddies.'

The priest felt his heart begin to thump in his chest and the blood rush to his face. 'I . . . I . . .' He was lost for words.

'Now come along,' said the park-keeper, placing a hand on the priest's arm. 'You go and find somewhere else to sit.'

Chapter Two

'Father McKenzie.'

The priest was staring at the stain on the wall in the Lady Chapel. It was like the cancer inside him, he thought, silent, unstoppable, slowly spreading. The incident in the park had upset him. Couldn't you look at children these days without people thinking you had some deeper, darker motive for doing so? 'People might get the wrong idea,' the park-keeper had said.

'Father McKenzie.'

He glanced around. It was Miss Evans, his housekeeper. She looked like a vulture, with the sagging skin around the neck, the large beak of a nose and the red-rimmed eyes.

'Ah, Miss Evans,' he said, giving her a friendly smile.

'You were miles away.'

'Yes, I was.'

'It's time for confession, Father,' she said. 'There's a queue.'

She sounded like a schoolmistress reminding a forgetful child.

'Thank you,' he said simply. He made the sign of the cross and, pulling himself to his feet, headed for the side chapel.

For the next hour he sat in the black box hidden behind a small grille, listening to people telling him about their sins. It was always the same stories. 'I said some unkind words,' 'I've been mean,' 'I've been selfish,' 'I've had bad thoughts about somebody,' 'I lost my temper,' 'I shouted at the kids.' There was never a murder or an armed robbery, thank God.

It wasn't much of a queue—just three or four women sitting in the nearest pew and a nervous young man, perhaps about thirty years old, who sat some distance away, biting his lip and fidgeting. The priest recognized the women. They were regulars and they would confess the same old sins.

The young man was different. Father McKenzie hadn't seen him before, but he had come across troubled young men like him. They hoped that this unseen listener in the darkness of the confessional might have the answer to their problems. Of course, the priest rarely had the answer.

When the women had gone Father McKenzie waited in the musty little box for the young man to enter. He sat in the darkness, thinking about the interview at the hospital and what he would write in his letter to the bishop. Finally he heard the door on the other side of the confessional open and close with a click.

'I need some help, some advice,' came a voice from the other side of the grille. 'I need to talk to somebody.' In the semi-darkness the priest made out the shape of the young man.

'Do you wish me to hear your confession?' asked the priest.

'I'm not a catholic.'

'That doesn't matter. I'm a good listener.'

'I just needed to talk to somebody.'

'Of course.'

'I've no one else I can talk to.'

'Would you like to tell me what troubles you?'

'It's difficult to explain.'

'Take your time.'

'Perhaps I'd better go,' said the young man.

'You don't need to,' said the priest gently. 'Just sit here for a while. It's a good place to think.'

The young man sniffed. 'I really don't know what to do.'

'Would you like to tell me about it?'

'I've no one else to talk to,' said the man. 'No one.'

'Everything you say in here will go no further,' said the priest. 'Nobody will know about our conversation.

Priests aren't allowed to tell what is said in the confessional. It's one of the rules.'

'It's not really sunk in yet,' said the young man. 'You know, you go through life, getting up in the morning to go to work. You go out with your mates, meet girls, watch the football on Saturday and everything seems fine. Then out of the blue you learn something that knocks the legs from under you.' The priest knew exactly what he meant but stayed silent for a while.

'My mother, God rest her soul,' the priest told him, 'always said we should expect the unexpected, that life is full of surprises.'

'Yes, well, I wasn't expecting this little surprise, I can tell you.'

'Are you ill?' the priest asked gently.

'No. I've just learnt something and it's come as a bombshell.'

'I see.' The priest didn't pry. He knew that if he remained quiet the young man might open up.

'I've just found out,' said the young man suddenly, 'that I was adopted. Thirty-three years old and I've only just discovered that the people who brought me up, and who I thought were my parents, adopted me when I was a baby. They never told me. They let me grow up thinking all the time that I was their own child.'

'You *were* their child,' said the priest simply.

'No, not really theirs.'

'Were they good parents?'

'Yes.'

'Did they love you, take care of you, tuck you in at night, read stories to you, help you with your schoolwork? Were they there for you when you were sick?'

'Yes, yes,' said the young man, 'they were, and I suppose I should be grateful for that.'

'Very grateful,' said the priest. 'They sound like very special parents to me.'

15

'But they lied to me,' said the young man. 'They let me go on believing that they were my real mother and father. Why didn't they tell me when I was young? Why did I have to find out now? Why did I have to find out like this?'

'I don't have an answer to that,' the priest told him.

'I thought you people were supposed to have the answers,' said the young man.

Father McKenzie gave a small laugh. 'If only that were the case, my son,' he said. 'How simple life would be.'

'I just can't understand why my mother decided to tell me now, why she kept it from me.'

'I'm sure that your parents felt they had a good reason to keep it from you.'

'Well, I can't understand why.'

'You say your parents were good parents.'

'They were,' the young man said

sadly.

'My guess is that they never wanted to lie to you. They were probably too scared to tell you. Perhaps they felt you might change if you found out the truth or that it might upset you too much. They maybe thought your feelings towards them would alter. There are many reasons why people act the way they do. They might have been waiting for the right time and somehow it never came around.'

'It was wrong not to tell me,' said the young man, wiping his eyes.

'Maybe it was.'

'There's no maybe about it. I should have been told the truth. I feel betrayed. All those times people said I'd got my father's eyes or my mother's smile, and they never said anything.'

'It's difficult, but try not to judge them too harshly.'

The young man snorted.

'How did you discover the truth?'

17

asked the priest.

'My mother just came out with it. Dad, well, I knew him as my dad, died a couple of years ago and she got it into her head that she should make a will. We had just got back from the solicitor's and she said I should sit down because there was something she needed to tell me. "Mark," she said. "Your dad and me should have told you before. We wanted to tell you so many times, but we put it off." I had no idea what she was talking about and then she said, "Mark, love, you were adopted when you were a baby."' The young man put his head in his hands. 'I can't tell you how empty I feel inside. How lonely I feel at this moment. I really don't know who I am or what to do.'

'I can't say whether your mother and father were right or wrong in not telling you the truth,' said the priest, 'but it is clear to me that they loved you very much and they have done their very best for you. Try to understand how difficult it is for your mother at this moment, what she is going through. She needs you more than ever now.'

'I can't speak to her,' said the young man. 'I just walked out. I said I needed to think things over.'

'Have you wondered why your mother chose this time to tell you?'

'No.'

'Perhaps she feels now that she's nearing the end of her life. Perhaps she needs to be honest, to tell you something that's been troubling her for years. She could have kept quiet, let you go on thinking she was the woman who gave birth to you, and gone to her grave with the secret.'

'It would have been better for her and for me if she had kept it to herself,' said the young man.

'No,' said the priest. 'She had to tell you before she died. She knows and has always known in her heart that you have a right to know. It's just that she left it a little late to tell you. When you've had time to think things through, you need to go back and talk to your mother.'

'I wouldn't know what to say to her.'

'The words will come. She loves you as much as any good mother and she needs you now.' There was a silence. 'I guess you are thinking about the woman who gave birth to you,' said the priest. 'Who she is and what she's like?'

'Yes,' replied the young man quietly. 'I've thought about it a lot.'

'And why she couldn't look after you?'

'You mean why she gave me away,' said the young man sharply.

'It's not quite as simple as that,' said the priest. 'There are many reasons why she could have given you up for adoption. Perhaps she just couldn't cope; perhaps she knew she couldn't give her baby the best start in life. She could have been a young unmarried woman, frightened, lonely, pressured by her parents who felt the disgrace keenly. It happened a lot. Nowadays people don't tend to get bothered about it. It's my guess that that young woman will have thought about you every day of her life, wondering what you are like and what you have made of yourself.'

'I don't think so,' said the young man. 'She's probably never given me a second thought.'

'I think you know that's not true,' the priest told him. 'The bond between mother and child is too strong. In time you might wish to trace your birth mother.'

'I don't think so,' said the young man. He sighed noisily. 'I had better go.'

'Before you do,' said the priest, 'just remember that your adoptive mother and father will have longed for a child of their own. Try to imagine the happiness they must

21

have felt when you came along, the happiness that you brought into their lives. Try to recall the love you have received from them, their joy on your success, the sacrifices they made. I ask you again not to judge them too harshly.'

'Thanks for listening,' said the young man dismissively.

'I will pray for you,' the priest told him.

The man gave a small grunt. 'I'm sorry, but I'm not a great believer in prayer.'

'You should try it,' said the priest. 'Prayer can be very powerful. Remember, I'm always here if you want to talk, Mark. I hope things work out for you.'

When the young man had gone, the priest bowed his head. He joined his fingers slowly and set them beneath his chin like a child at prayer.

'Oh Lord, who has united our

hearts in love,
Give us the joy to always love each
  other
And help this troubled young
  man.'

Coming out of the confessional box and into the bright sunlight, the priest was met by Miss Evans, the housekeeper. She held a broom like a rifle over her chest.

'You had better come with me, Father McKenzie,' she said, 'and see what some dirty individual has done in the church porch.'

Chapter Three

'Go on, off with you! You shouldn't be in here.'

Father McKenzie was up a ladder in the Lady Chapel examining the spreading stain above the altar. He heard the voice echoing down the church. Having climbed down, he went towards the noise to find Miss Evans stabbing a bony finger at a small wiry boy.

The child was a grubby little individual of about ten or eleven, with black bristly hair standing up like a lavatory brush. As the priest came closer, he noticed something small and green in the child's crusty nostril, dirty hands and shabby clothes. The boy had large dark eyes.

'What is it, Miss Evans?' he asked.

'I found this boy in the church, Father,' the housekeeper informed him angrily. 'He was skulking near the charity box.'

'I wasn't doing nothing!' shouted the child.

'Up to no good, I'm sure,' she said. 'Probably looking for something to steal.'

'That's a bloody lie!' cried the child.

'Don't you dare swear in the house of God!' snapped the housekeeper. 'Go on, off you go.'

'All right, Miss Evans,' said the priest. 'I'll deal with this.'

'He shouldn't be in here, Father,' the woman said. 'It's the likes of him who urinated in the holy water font in the porch.'

'What's she mean?' the child asked the priest.

'Someone went to the toilet in the holy water kept in the porch,' explained the priest.

'Dirty devils!' snapped the housekeeper.

'I never pissed in no holy water,'

said the child, his eyes bright with anger. He looked the priest straight in the face. It was strange, thought Father McKenzie, how adults, when talking to him, very often stared over his shoulders, almost afraid of making any eye contact, but this child looked straight at him, eyeball to eyeball.

'Well, I never did,' said the housekeeper. 'Will you listen to that? I've a good mind—'

'Miss Evans,' said the priest firmly, 'I said I would deal with it.'

'Very well, Father,' the housekeeper said, and she strode off down the aisle, mumbling angrily to herself.

'Are you her dad?' asked the boy.

'No,' laughed the priest, 'I am not her dad.'

'I didn't think you was. She's old enough to be *your* mother. She looks as if she's been dug up. Why did she call you father?'

'Well, I'm a priest and that is what

catholic priests are called.'

'Sounds daft to me, calling someone father and they've no kids.'

'It's a sort of title,' the priest told him. 'I'm the father of the people who come to my church.'

The boy looked around him. 'Not many, then,' he said bluntly.

'Sadly, not.'

'I wasn't going to nick anything, you know,' said the boy.

'I am sure you weren't,' said the priest.

'I was just looking.'

'That's all right. Take your time.'

'People always think that I'm up to no good. I bet if I was dressed like one of them kids from that posh school, with a red blazer and a cap on my head, and talked la-di-bloody-da, that old bag would have left me alone.'

'You know you ought not to swear,' said the priest.

'Call that swearing!' cried the boy.

He laughed and wiped his nose on the back of his hand. 'You should hear my mam and her boyfriend when they're having one of their rows. I get out of the house when they get started and I come in here. I like it in here.' He stared up at the roof. 'It's quiet and there are no people about. You can just sit here on a bench and nobody bothers you. I like the pictures on the walls as well, and the smell. What *is* that smell?'

'It's incense,' the priest told him.

'What's that then?'

'It's a sort of spice that when it's burned gives off a sweet smell, a sort of perfume. When baby Jesus was born, one of the three kings brought Him a gift of incense. It was very precious. The other two kings brought gold and myrrh. Have you not been in a nativity play at school?'

'A what?'

'A play about the time when Jesus was born.'

'When I was a little kid, I was,' the child told him. 'I was a palm tree. I had to stand on the stage wearing this stupid brown crêpe paper wrapped round me and green cardboard leaves on my head, holding these plastic coconuts. I looked a right prat. People started laughing at me. I didn't know what to do. I was dead scared and I wet myself. The teacher gave me a right telling off.'

The priest raised an eyebrow. 'Oh dear.'

'It came through the paper, see, in this big brown stain, and everybody started laughing at me again. Then bits fell off and they could see my underpants. They were bright blue. I started crying and came off the stage. The teacher told me to go back on, but I told her to get stuffed and went home. What's it for?'

'What is what for?' asked the priest.

'The incense.'

'Well, it makes the church smell rather special, and when it's lit, the smoke rises to the roof and reminds us of our prayers rising to God.'

'I don't believe in God,' said the child bluntly, 'but I just like coming here.'

'You've been in the church before then?'

'Oh yeah, loads of times, and it wasn't me what pissed in the holy water.'

The priest smiled. 'Yes, you told me that.'

'And I've never nicked nothing either.'

'I'm sure you haven't.'

'I have nicked stuff but I wouldn't nick it from here.'

'You shouldn't steal things, you know,' said the priest. 'It doesn't matter whether it's from here or not. It's wrong. You should be a good boy.'

'I'm not being a good boy,' replied the boy. 'It don't get you anywhere.'

He pointed down the church to the great hanging crucifix. 'I mean, He was a good boy, wasn't He, Jesus, and look where He ended up.' The priest smiled. He was a little character, this one, he thought. 'It wants painting, this church,' said the child. 'It's beginning to look tatty.'

'Yes, it is,' agreed Father McKenzie.

'My dad was a painter and decorator. He buggered off when I was little. He's in the nick now. I never see him. My mam never talks about him.'

'Where do you live?' asked the priest.

'Brightwood Terrace. It's crap. Nothing there but waste land, mucky streets, burned-out cars, rubbish all over the place, writing on the walls. That's why I like to come in here. There's no noise. It's like a sort of old palace, with all these colours and statues. Sometimes, when the sun

31

shines through them windows, it's like a rainbow. I like to sit underneath it. I close my eyes and go into another world.'

The priest looked around him. Some palace, he thought, with its dimly lit rows of dark scarred pews, cold tiled floor, rusty red heating pipes, ugly liver-coloured brickwork and windows high and thin. Then there was the flaking paint and that dark, creeping stain.

'I'm Father McKenzie,' he said.

'I'm Matthew, but my mam calls me Matty when she's in a good mood and "little bugger" when she's not.'

'Well, Matthew. You stay here as long as you want. When you've finished, close the door in the porch when you go.'

'Can I come back, then?'

'Yes.'

'That old biddy won't kick me out?'

'No.'

The child sniffed noisily and wiped

his nose again on the back of his hand. 'You're all right, you,' he said.

The priest smiled. 'So are you,' he replied.

Chapter Four

The following Saturday Father McKenzie felt a sharp pain in his side as he sat in the confessional box. He took a deep breath. Perhaps he should have taken some of the tablets the doctor had given him.

It was a tiring hour for the priest that morning. One of the women, the world-weary Mrs Leary, a huge woman with a loud voice, complained about her husband who wanted his 'conjugal rights' every week. She wanted to know what to do when he came in the worse for drink, smelling of beer and cigarettes, and climbed into bed on top of her. Father McKenzie pictured the scene. He told her it was her duty as a wife not to deny her husband, but perhaps she ought to discuss the situation with him. He could tell that it was not what the woman wanted to hear.

'You want to try talking to the big fat lump, Father, when he comes in drunk as a lord, smelling of beer and groping me like an octopus.'

The next person to speak to him, Mrs Wilson, spent a good ten minutes telling the priest all about her many ailments before going on about her difficult neighbours and the youth of the day. She was a sad, lonely and bitter woman.

The priest liked the last regular, Miss Rigby, and he looked forward to her visits. She was a quiet, rather nervous woman, shabbily dressed in an old black coat and knitted woollen hat. She wore too much make-up, and smiled with bright red lips and blinked rapidly with heavily black-lined eyes. Miss Rigby was the only one who ever asked him how he was and thanked him for his time and trouble. She never complained, and had few sins to confess. Although she never said so, it was clear to Father McKenzie that she was lonely, like many of the people who came to see him, and just wanted someone to talk to. The priest always had time for her.

'I was wondering, Father,' she whispered through the grille that morning, 'if you might say a special mass for me.'

'Of course,' said the priest. 'Is it for a special intention?'

'It's for someone special. It will be his birthday on Thursday,' she added. 'I think about him a lot. I called him Matthew. I was told it means "Gift of God". It won't be his name now, of course.'

'It would be my pleasure to say a mass for you, Miss Rigby,' said the priest.

A small white envelope was slid through from the other side of the confessional box. 'There's some money in here,' she said.

'No, no, Miss Rigby,' said the priest, sliding the envelope back. 'You hang on to your savings. I say mass every day and will make Thursday's mass your special one.'

'You're a good man, Father McKenzie,' said the woman. 'A good man.'

The priest waited for her to go, but she stayed where she was.

'Was there something else?' he asked.

'The birthday, Father,' she said.

'Yes?'

'He will be sixty on Thursday. Matthew, my son.'

'Your son?' the priest repeated.

'I had a son, Father.' He heard her sniff. 'I gave him up.'

'I see,' said the priest.

'I was only sixteen. I was young. I fell in love. I was innocent. To be honest, I didn't really know what was happening. My parents never talked about that sort of thing, you know, the facts of life. My father was so mad when I told him. I've never seen him so angry. The shame I had brought on the family, he said, an unmarried mother. He was quite an important man in the town, well known, and he said I had disgraced him. He said he would never forgive me. He wanted me to get rid of the baby but I wouldn't. I couldn't. They hushed things up, my parents. I was sent to an aunt in Devon, as far away from gossiping neighbours as they could find. He was so beautiful, my baby, with a big, big smile and soft white hair like feathers. He had little nails like pink seashells. I only held him once, stroked his little head, kissed him and then he was taken from me.'

'The child was adopted?' asked the priest.

'Yes, he was adopted. Somebody else took him, fed him and changed him and watched him grow up. I went home. I felt so empty. Life went on. My parents never mentioned it again.'

'It was hard for you,' said the priest quietly.

'Oh, Father,' said the woman. 'It was far worse than hard. It broke my heart.'

The priest thought of Mark, the troubled young man. He wondered if the young woman who had given birth to him and given him up for adoption felt as this poor, sad, lonely woman kneeling before him felt. He thought of another Matthew, the neglected little boy who came into the church.

'I went to work in my father's office,' the woman told him, 'and tried to put my baby out of my mind but I couldn't. I used to look at children and imagine what my baby would be looking like as he grew up. I lived with my parents, looked after them, and when they became old and ill I nursed them until they died. I knew the others in the office felt sorry for me—shy little Miss Rigby who's never had a boyfriend, has no friends, the only one who never comes to the office parties. Poor

Miss Rigby in her old-fashioned clothes, with her boring life. I knew what they said about me. None of them knew, of course, about the baby.' She blew her nose noisily. 'Do you know, Father, a day doesn't pass when I don't think about him and what he's like now. If he's been a success in life, if he has children of his own.'

'And you never thought of trying to trace your son?' asked the priest.

'Yes, of course. I've thought about it often but I was frightened. What could I say to someone I had given away? What would he have to say to me after all this time? How would he have felt? His new parents may not have told him he was adopted, so think of all the trouble it would cause, me turning up on his doorstep and saying, "I'm your mother." I've waited, Father, in the hope that he may contact me, but I guess he never will.' The woman began to weep.

'I'll say the mass, Miss Rigby,' said

the priest sadly, 'and I will pray for you.'

*   *   *

'Hi,' said the boy as the priest came out of the confessional box. Father McKenzie felt dizzy and steadied himself on the nearest pew. 'Are you OK?'

'Yes, I'm fine.' He forced a bright smile. 'You should be out in the fresh air, Matthew, not inside on a lovely day like this.'

'I wanted to ask you something.' The boy's face was sharp, like a keen little rodent.

'Yes.'

'What are all these pictures round the walls? They're painted on blocks of white stone.'

'Those are the stations of the cross,' the priest told him. 'Come along, you can walk around the church with me and I'll explain.'

'Stations?' repeated the boy,

41

following in the priest's footsteps. 'They never had stations in those days.'

The priest laughed. 'Not railway stations. They tell the story of Jesus's journey to the cross. They remind us of His suffering.'

They stared for a moment at one of the tablets. Silently the priest repeated a prayer:

'O Jesus, who for the love of me
Didst bear the cross to Calvary,
In thy sweet mercy grant to me
To suffer and to die with thee.'

'They killed Him, didn't they?' the boy said after a while.

'Yes, they killed Him,' said the priest. He pointed to one of the painted tablets on the wall. 'They mocked Him, laughed at Him, whipped Him, wrapped an old piece of purple rag around Him and called Him "King of the Jews". They challenged Him to show them that

He was in fact the Son of God and had all this power. Had He wanted, He could have turned them into dust beneath His sandals.'

'And He let them do it to Him?'

'He did.'

'Why?'

'Because He came into the world to help and heal people, not to hurt them.'

'I'd have hurt them if they'd have done it to me,' said the boy.

'I guess many of us would have,' the priest told him, 'but Jesus didn't.'

'Why did they kill Him if all He did was want to help them?'

Father McKenzie thought for a moment. 'They killed Him,' he said, 'because they hated Him. They were jealous of His power, thought He had hidden motives and maybe they were a little frightened of Him too. Does that make sense?'

The boy cocked his head to one side. 'I think so.'

'Is there anything else you want to

ask, Matthew?'

'Hadn't He got any friends?'

'He had, but they deserted Him when He needed them most. His best friend Peter said he didn't know Him three times when he was asked.'

'Some friends,' said the boy.

'They were frightened.'

'I haven't got any friends,' he said.

'No friends?' asked the priest.

'No.' The boy pointed to the wall. 'Then these soldiers nailed Him to that cross?'

'They did, but before that they forced a crown of sharp thorns on to His head and called him "King of the Jews".'

'The bastards,' said the child.

'Yes, I suppose they were,' agreed the priest, biting his lip to hide his smile, 'but that's not quite how I would put it.'

Miss Evans emerged though a side door. She pulled a face when she saw the boy.

'It's that old biddy,' whispered

the boy.

'Matthew,' said Father McKenzie, 'that's not very nice.'

'Well, she doesn't like me, and she has a mouth all screwed up as tight as a duck's arse.'

The priest shook his head. 'Matthew, if I let you come into the church you mustn't speak like that. It's very rude.'

'Father McKenzie, there you are,' said the housekeeper. 'I wondered where you had got to. Your lunch is ready.'

'I was just telling young Matthew here,' said the priest, 'about the stations of the cross.' He didn't really need to explain himself to her, but felt somehow he had to.

'I see,' she said. 'Well, ought he not to be getting home?'

'Yes, I think so,' agreed the priest. 'Off you go, Matthew.'

'Can I come again, then?'

'Of course.'

The housekeeper shook her head.

45

Chapter Five

Lunch was one of Miss Evans's special dishes—hotpot. Father McKenzie felt sick as he saw the food being spooned on to his plate: grey lumps of meat, slices of blue-edged potato, overcooked carrots, pale onions, and all swimming in a greasy lake.

'I'm not too hungry, actually, Miss Evans,' he said, pushing the plate aside.

'Not hungry!' she cried. 'You're not ill, are you, Father?'

Perhaps this was the time to tell her, he thought, but he decided to wait. He would let the bishop know first. 'No, no, I'm fine, just a little tired. I didn't sleep well last night.'

'You didn't touch the fish I cooked yesterday,' she told him.

The very thought of the half-cooked square of haddock in the sticky white sauce, sprinkled with sprigs of limp parsley and served with lumpy potatoes and bullet-hard peas, brought a sour taste to his mouth.

'You don't look well, Father,' said the housekeeper. 'You've been overdoing it.'

'I think I've a touch of the flu that's going round,' the priest told her.

'You can pick up all sorts in that confessional box,' she said, removing the plate. 'It must be a hotbed of germs in there.'

'It was rather stuffy,' agreed the priest.

'I see that Mrs Wilson was at confession again. How you put up with her I don't know, Father. She's got every illness under the sun, that woman. She stopped me in the porch when I was cleaning out the font and went on and on about her medical problems. I said to her, I said, "Mrs Wilson, you should get down on your

47

knees and thank God you're still on your feet." Some people never stop complaining.'

Father McKenzie smiled. 'Well, I guess she's very lonely. The world is full of lonely people, Miss Evans. One wonders where they all come from.'

'I see that Miss Rigby was there as usual,' the housekeeper said. 'She's so holy, that woman, she bites the altar rails. She looks terrible ill though, doesn't she, poor woman? As my mother would say, she has the smell of clay on her. She's not long for this world, that's for sure.'

Another lonely person, thought the priest.

'She gets more and more odd, in that old coat and knitted hat like a tea cosy and those big brown boots and clutching that plastic carrier bag. Come rain or shine, winter or summer, she's always dressed the same and always with that plastic bag. Last week, after that wedding, she was outside the church picking up the rice, grain by grain. I mean, whatever does she want with little bits of rice? She must be living in a dream.'

The priest sighed but said nothing.

'I didn't see any sign of Mrs Hardy,' said the housekeeper.

'No, she wasn't at confession,' said the priest. 'I must telephone her and see how her husband is. Poor man looked so ill when I saw him last week.'

'There's no need,' said the housekeeper. 'I saw her in the post office yesterday collecting his pension. I asked after him, of course, thinking that that would be the last pension she'd be collecting, what with him being at death's door. I thought it wouldn't be long before she'd be in touch with you to arrange the funeral and, blow me down, she said he's up and about. Would you believe it?'

'That's good to hear,' said the

priest.

'Your visit must have put the very fear of God into him,' said the housekeeper, 'because after you'd gone, he was out of bed howling healthy and raring to go, asking for two fried eggs, three rashers of bacon and a black pudding. On Saturday he was down at the "Golden Ball" drinking ale with the best of them. As like as not he'll be running the London marathon next week, as large as life and twice as natural.'

'I'm very pleased,' said the priest, rising from the table. 'Well, I have a sermon to prepare for tomorrow.' I also have a letter to compose to the bishop, he thought to himself. The housekeeper remained by the door, holding the plate. 'Is there something else, Miss Evans?'

'About that boy,' she said.

'Yes?'

'That grubby little boy who was in the church.'

'I know who you mean,' said the priest. 'His name is Matthew. What about him?'

'Well, I've seen him hanging about in the church before.'

'He likes to come here,' the priest told her.

'Far be it from me to interfere, Father McKenzie, but if I was you, I wouldn't encourage him. No good will come of it.'

'He's just a child, Miss Evans,' said the priest, 'only a child. I feel rather sorry for him. He's a lonely little boy and has a poor home life it seems.'

'Well, if you ask me, I reckon he's up to no good, wandering around the empty church. One of these days you'll find the brass candlesticks missing from your altar, your walls covered in graffiti and the holy water in the porch font smelling like a sewer again. You mark my words.'

'I think at heart he's a good lad,' said the priest, 'and he's a clever little boy, quite a chatty child. He has a lot about him. Looking at him, I don't suppose he gets much attention at home.'

'Mmm,' she hummed, with that well-fancy-that sort of smile. 'I really don't think you should be letting him come into the church, if you don't mind me saying.'

'As I said, he seems to like it here,' the priest told her. 'It's quiet and calming and he's interested in the things around him.'

'Interested in what he can steal, I bet,' she said.

'I think you're being a little unkind, Miss Evans,' said the priest quietly.

The housekeeper's mouth closed into a tight little line. 'Well, that may be, Father, but I was having a word with the woman behind the counter in the post office and she knows him. I was telling her about how he keeps turning up in the church. Matthew Brown's his name. Mrs Leary says he's a right little tearaway. Always in some sort of trouble. He's stolen things from the post office, sweets and crisps. He lives on that big estate where all the trouble is. Mrs Wilson, who was in the post office as well, says his family is a bad lot. Father in prison, mother never in, and when she is, she brings men home. She lets him wander the streets getting up to all sorts of mischief. I mean, you can see what sort of home he's from. He wants a good wash for a start and some of the words he comes out with would make a soldier blush.'

'Suffer little children,' said the priest quietly.

'I beg your pardon?'

'Luke, Chapter 18,' Father McKenzie told her. ' "Suffer little children to come unto me," said Jesus, "and do not hinder them, for the kingdom of God belongs to these. I tell you this, anyone who will not receive a little child will never enter the kingdom of heaven." '

'Don't say you haven't been warned, Father McKenzie. That's all I'll say,' the housekeeper told him. 'I'll get your coffee.'

Chapter Six

Father McKenzie did not sleep much that night. He thought of the grubby little boy who found the church so interesting. He too, like little Matthew, had loved going into a church when he was a child. He liked the colours, the ornaments, the coolness, the statues and the mass, chanted in a language centuries old. It was a dimly lit little chapel, smelling of damp, old wood and incense, with the rain beating at the stained-glass windows. He had watched the altar boys in red and white walk in front of the priest, one holding a great cross before him and the others bearing lighted candles. It had been magical.

He remembered going to mass as a child with his parents, dressed in his Sunday best. There was a picture of him his mother kept on the sideboard, showing him smiling at the camera. He was in grey shorts, with shiny, black, tight-fitting shoes, stockings pulled up to the knees, white shirt with the tight collar and clip-on tie. As the people filed out at the end of mass, he would go to the plaster statue of the pale-faced Virgin Mary in her blue robe and kneel before her. At the brass candle shrine to the side of the altar, he would buy a penny candle and make a silent wish. Let me be a priest, he would pray.

As he lay there now in the darkness, scenes of his childhood grew around him. He could see his mother, full of life and laughter, moving around the farmhouse kitchen, speaking rapidly, stroking his head gently as she passed with a kind word. She would read to him every night, and he came to love words and swam in an ocean of language.

He watched his mother a lot when

he was small. She never knew he was looking at her as she went busily about her work. He saw her feed a stray cat and scatter bread for the birds, and learnt that it was good to be kind to other creatures. He watched her bake gingerbread men with currant buttons, and learnt that the little things in life are sometimes more important than the big things. He watched her ironing and singing to herself, saw her smiling and wanted to smile like that too.

Sometimes he saw her cry, and learnt that things in the world did hurt but that it was all right to cry. He saw her on her knees praying, and learnt that there was a God to whom he could talk as well. He saw her sitting on the front row in the school hall when he was in the infant nativity play and heard her clap the loudest when he took his bow. He learnt then what it felt like to be proud. When she kissed him goodnight and told him how special he was, he learnt the meaning of love.

As the priest lay there in the darkness of the room, he recalled his father. He had thick wavy black hair and shining blue eyes and a handsome face. He could picture him standing in the farmyard among the ploughs and mowing machines, watching the swallows swooping and darting above him. His father was not a man who showed any signs of affection like his mother. He might sometimes ruffle his son's hair, put an arm around his shoulder and peck him on the cheek before he went to bed, but this stopped when his son's age reached double figures.

It was a happy childhood. He was a quiet, well-behaved boy, an only child and a bit of a loner at school. At home he helped muck out the pigs, tidy the hay in the barn, gather the eggs and feed the chickens without grumbling. Up at six, he helped feed and milk the cows. After that he washed and changed into his school clothes. Then he went down for breakfast and, with his satchel packed, he walked the two miles to the Christian Brothers' College. Back from school at five, he ate a slice of bread and jam and then it was back to work on the farm. It was expected of him and he didn't complain, but he was keen to get to his books, to start his homework and to read.

When he told his parents he wanted to be a priest, there was an argument. His mother, he knew, had always hoped that he would become a priest and he could picture her face glowing with pride when he told her. His father was against it from the start and tried to 'make him see sense'. Who would take over the farm? What about grandchildren? Did he not know what a lonely life a priest led? Then the shouting started. His father blamed the teachers up at the school, for putting silly ideas into his head. He listened quietly to his father's angry words, watched him banging his heavy fist on the table and then storming out of the kitchen. There was a cold silence over the next few days, but he had not changed his mind. He would become a priest.

He returned to the farm after his father's death and found it run down and deserted, with weeds sprouting from the broken guttering and the once shining whitewashed walls now a dirty grey. The windows were broken and an overgrown arch of roses covered the door. As the darkness gathered, rooks flapped in the air like scraps of black cloth floating on the wind.

After his training he went back to the village near to where he had grown up. The old parish priest, Father Walsh, welcomed this keen young man and gave him much of the day-to-day work to do. Father McKenzie happily took it on.

The young priest became a regular visitor to the small school in the village. The head teacher, Miss Martin, a cold woman with hooded eyes and a scowl, was not at all keen on him calling in. She had been left alone by old Father Walsh and liked a quiet life.

'The children's reading isn't very good,' Father McKenzie told her after spending a day in the school.

'Well, no, it isn't,' agreed the head teacher, 'but look where these children come from. I mean, what can you expect of them? Books are not part of their lives. The only book some of them have in the house is the big yellow one kept by the telephone.'

'It's very important for them to learn to read,' said the young priest.

'Is it?' asked the head teacher.

'Well, of course,' the priest told her, surprised. 'A person who cannot read is held back in life. Books are the windows on the world.'

'These are farming children,' said the head teacher. The priest could tell by her tone of voice that she was not pleased with what he had said. 'All they are bothered about is leaving school to work on the farm. You don't need to be a good reader to look after pigs and cattle and sheep.'

'I was born on a farm,' said the priest. 'I came from a farming family.'

The head teacher frowned. 'Well, perhaps your parents wanted something better for you and took an interest in what you did in school. The parents of these children just want them to leave school and help on the farm.'

Father McKenzie thought of his own father, but he said nothing.

Chapter Seven

When he was a young priest in Ireland, Father McKenzie started to call in at the small school each week, despite the coldness of the head teacher and the two sour-faced members of staff. They felt that he was meddling with their work. Each morning he sat with the children who struggled with their reading, listening to them and talking about the books.

The first child who came to see him on his first visit was a small rosy-cheeked boy with wiry blond hair and large brown eyes. He was not keen on having to come and see the priest, who was sitting waiting in the small Reading Corner. He eyed the square of carpet and the old bookshelf.

'I can't go on the carpet,' the child told him flatly.

'You can,' said the priest.

'No, I can't. I can't go on that

carpet.'

'Did someone say you couldn't go on the carpet?'

'No, but I'm not going on it!'

'Why?'

'Because I'm not!'

'Is there some reason why you can't go on the carpet?' the priest asked.

'Aye, there is.'

'Well, why can't you go on the carpet?'

'Because I've got shit on my shoe.'

'You must not say that word,' the priest told him.

The child stared at the priest. 'What word?' he asked.

'The "s" word.'

'Shoe?'

'The other.'

'Shit?'

'You mustn't say it.'

'Why?'

'Because it's not a very nice word for a little boy to use.'

'Why?'

'Well, it's just not a nice word to use, that's all.'

'Well, what word should I use then?'

'Just say you've got dirt on your shoe.'

'But it's not dirt, is it? It's shit.'

Oh dear, thought the priest.

'Anyway,' said the child, 'my dad uses it all the time on the farm.'

The teacher, a stern-faced woman with steely grey hair scraped back on her scalp, appeared. 'Is Liam giving you trouble, Father?' she asked.

'No,' said the priest. 'No trouble.'

'He can be a very cheeky boy,' said the teacher, looking at him like a bird of prey watching its next meal. 'Can't you, Liam?'

The child looked up at her with narrowed eyes but said nothing.

'He's being very good today,' the priest told her.

'Is he?' asked the teacher. 'Well, that will make a change.'

When the teacher had gone he

turned back to the boy. 'What does your mum say if you have it on your shoe?' he asked.

'Have what on my shoe?'

'You know what.' He pointed to his feet.

'She makes me take my shoes off.'

'Well, take them off, Liam, get your reading book and come into the Reading Corner with me.'

The boy went to his desk and returned clutching a dog-eared book. He had taken off his shoes and the priest noticed the holes in his old socks. The child had an earthy smell about him. The book he held was called *Dan and Nan Have Fun*.

'I'll read to you now if you want,' he said, 'but I'm no good. I'm a slow reader and I can't make out some of the words.'

'Don't worry about that,' said the priest, smiling. 'Just try your best.'

'I'll come on the carpet now because I've taken off my shoes.'

'Right,' said the priest.

The reading book was old with a crumpled grey cover. It did not appear to offer much fun. The boy screwed up his eyes and frowned. He read the words slowly.

'Here is Dan.
Dan is a boy.
Here is Nan.
Nan is a girl.
Dan is a boy.
Nan is a girl.
Dan is Nan's brother.
Nan is Dan's sister.
They have fun.
Here is a house.
Dan and Nan live in the house.
They live near a river.
They have fun.
Dan has a canoe.
Dan and Nan go in the canoe.
They go on the river.
Dan paddles the canoe.
They have fun.
Nan sings a song.
Dan catches a fish.

Dan chops some wood.
Dan lights a fire.
Nan cooks the fish.
They eat the fish.
They have fun.'

The pictures showed a clean little boy dressed in his school blazer and cap. He wore a white shirt, a neatly knotted tie, highly polished shoes and knee-length socks.

'He's not dressed for a fishing trip, is he?' said the priest. 'He looks as if he's going to church.'

Nan was dressed in a colourful frock, bright blue shoes and dazzling white stockings, and she had great red ribbons in her long blonde plaits. She, like her brother, looked very happy.

'And this young lady looks as if she's off to a party,' said the priest.

'I thought you wanted me to read to you?' asked the boy.

'I do,' said the priest.

The child read on slowly, stopping

at each word.

'That's not too bad, Liam,' said the priest when he had finished.

'Who are you kidding?' the boy said. 'I'm rubbish.'

'You do try very hard,' said the priest, thinking what a pity it was that the book was so dry and dreary. 'What do you think of the story?' he asked.

'It's stupid!' He shook his head. 'I mean, going in a canoe on a fast-flowing river is asking for trouble, and you'd never catch a trout in them waters with that rod. He wouldn't catch a cold with that. As for chopping wood up with that great big axe. Well, where did that come from? He could have taken his fingers off. I wouldn't let him loose with a penknife, never mind a ruddy great axe. And another thing, you should never light fires near a forest. They want to get some work done, them two, instead of pratting about all day having fun. I have to collect eggs on our farm, feed sows, fill troughs and coop up hens before my tea.'

'I did too when I was your age,' the priest told him.

'You did?'

'I was born on a farm. I used to have to do all those jobs and then I would get a book.'

'I don't like reading,' said the boy.

'Perhaps, if I brought you some more interesting books, you might like it more.'

'Maybe,' said the child. He paused and looked around him and sniffed the air. 'Can you smell anything?' he asked.

'No,' replied the priest.

'I can,' said the boy. 'I reckon I've got shit on my socks as well.'

With that he walked away.

*　　　　*　　　　*

Father McKenzie lay there thinking of the past. He wondered whatever happened to that small rosy-cheeked boy with the wiry blond hair. He probably ended up on the farm, he thought, and was never able to read very well.

After he had made a few visits to the school, Father McKenzie had been called into Father Walsh's study one evening. The old priest had smiled and told him that the head teacher had complained.

'I know you are a keen young man, Father McKenzie,' he was told, 'and that you think you are doing some good by calling in at the school, but you are making the head teacher and the staff nervous. I think you should leave the teaching of the children to them, don't you?'

Father McKenzie tried to put his side of the story, that the children were learning little and that the head teacher and her staff were little better than useless. They expected nothing from the children except that they keep quiet. The books they were given were old and boring. The children deserved better. Father Walsh listened, but it was clear that the visits to the school had to stop.

'What you say may very well be right, Father,' said the old priest, 'but this is a small village. Everyone knows everyone else, most are related and people do not like change. You have to learn to fit in, not try and change things. So stay out of the school, there's a good fellow.'

It wasn't long before Father McKenzie was moved to a parish in England.

Chapter Eight

The housekeeper stood at the door of the priest's study. Her bony hands were clasped in front of her. She was tight-lipped.

Father McKenzie looked up from the papers on his desk. He had been reading through the sermon he had spent the morning writing, a sermon that no one would hear. 'Oh, Miss Evans,' he said, 'I didn't see you there. Was there something you wanted?'

'It's that boy,' she said.

'Boy?' repeated the priest.

'That grubby little urchin. He's outside. He wants to see you.'

Father McKenzie tidied the papers and removed his glasses. 'His name is Matthew,' he told her. 'You had better show the young man in.'

'What? In here?' she asked.

'Yes, in here, Miss Evans.'

'You want me to bring him in here, Father? Into your study?'

'Yes, I do,' replied the priest calmly. Then he added, 'If you would be so kind.'

The housekeeper made a loud clucking noise with her tongue and left.

Father McKenzie sighed. He really must have a word with her about her manner, he thought. It had become so sharp of late, and she spoke to him at times like a teacher talking to a naughty schoolboy.

She returned a moment later with the boy.

'Go on there,' she told him, 'and don't you go touching anything.'

The child had been crying. His eyes were red-rimmed and his cheeks were streaked with dirty marks where he had wiped away the tears. He looked tense and miserable as he stood in the doorway.

'Come in, Matthew,' said the priest.

The boy came into the room looking around, wide-eyed. 'I wanted to see you,' he said, sniffing.

'Sit down, Matthew,' said the priest gently, pointing to the old sofa.

The boy sat and leaned forward, putting his head in his hands. He looked bent, like a broken puppet. 'You're the only one I can talk to,' said the child, on the point of tears.

Father McKenzie came over, sat beside him and put his arm around the child's shoulder. 'Now what's all this?' he asked.

'It's my mam and Craig. I hate them.'

'Who's Craig?' asked the priest.

'My mam's new boyfriend. I hate him. He shouts all the time and he throws things. My mam tells me to keep out of his way because I get on his nerves. Nothing I do is ever right. He calls me a useless little bugger. I hate him and I hate my mam as well.'

'You don't mean that, Matthew,' said the priest.

75

'I do. I wish she wasn't my mam. She doesn't want me around. She never has. She told me once I was a waste of space like my dad and one day I'd end up in prison like him. She told me that she wished she'd never had me. She said she should have had me adopted when I was a baby.'

'People say things they don't mean, Matthew,' said the priest, 'when they are angry.'

'Naw, she said it when she wasn't angry.' The boy rubbed his eyes. 'Can I stay here with you for a bit? I don't want to go back.'

'No, Matthew,' said the priest, 'that wouldn't be a very good idea.'

'Why?'

'Because it's getting late and your mother will be worrying about you and be wondering where you are.'

'She won't. She couldn't care less. She's gone out to the pub with Craig anyway and won't be back until late. He'll be in a real mood when he gets in. He always is when he's drunk.'

The housekeeper appeared at the door. 'Have you finished, Father McKenzie?' she asked sharply.

'Not quite, Miss Evans,' he said. 'Perhaps you could get Matthew here a glass of milk and one of your biscuits?'

'Milk and biscuits,' she repeated.

'Yes, Miss Evans,' the priest told her in a weary tone of voice. 'Milk and biscuits.'

Her eyebrows arched above the close-set, unsmiling eyes. 'Very well, Father,' she said and left, leaving the door open.

'Why can't I stay here with you?' the boy asked. 'You're the only one who never shouts at me, who listens to me.' He looked the priest in the eyes. 'The only one who has any time for me. I can talk to you.'

'Has this Craig hit you?' asked the priest.

'No.'

'Are you sure?'

'No, he's all mouth. He shouts a

77

lot and gets drunk, but he's not hit me. I just wish I wasn't in the house. Can I stay here, please, just for a bit?'

'It's not possible for you to stay here, Matthew,' Father McKenzie told him. 'You have a home and a mother. I know it must be difficult for you at the moment but things will get better. Try to keep out of the way of your mother's boyfriend. You could stay in your room out of his way and read.'

'I'm no good at reading and I don't like books,' said the boy. 'I watch telly most of the time, and then I get shouted at for having it on too loud. He's always shouting at me, Craig. I hate him.'

'You are always welcome here, Matthew, at any time during the day, if you are not at school. You are going to school, aren't you?'

'Sometimes.'

'You must go to school, but at the weekend, if you want to talk to me, I shall always be here.'

The housekeeper returned with a tray which she placed noisily on the desk.

'Is there anything else, Father McKenzie?' she asked curtly.

'No, nothing else, Miss Evans, thank you.'

'Remember you've got mass at seven o'clock.'

'I haven't forgotten,' he replied.

She left the room without another word, closing the door noisily behind her.

The child gulped down the milk and ate the biscuits greedily.

'Now,' said the priest, 'I think it would be a good idea if you went on home.'

'I don't want to go,' said the child.

'It's getting dark and your mother will be worrying about you.'

'I told you, she'll be out,' said the child, getting up from the sofa. 'I suppose that makes it better though. Thanks for the milk and the biscuits.'

The priest went to the bookshelf and picked out a large picture book. 'I want you to have this book, Matthew,' he said. 'It belonged to me when I was your age. It's a bit old and the worse for wear, but it has some lovely coloured pictures in and the words aren't too hard.'

'What's it about?' asked the boy.

'It's the stories Jesus told. They are called parables. Will you try to read it?'

'All right,' said the child, taking the book from him. 'Do you want it back?'

'No, it's for you to keep.'

'I never get presents,' said the boy, stroking the cover. 'Thanks.'

After the boy had gone Father McKenzie thought for a moment and rubbed the pain in his side. What feeble advice he had given the child. Go back and put up with it. Perhaps he ought to alert Social Services. He would have to think what to do about Matthew. The priest turned to his desk and re-read his sermon: words, words, words! He tore up the papers. He would write another. He began scribbling: ' "From the lips of children and infants, You have ordained praise," it says in the psalms. Children deserve the best the world can give them,' he wrote. 'Some children are fortunate to have the very best, parents who love and cherish them, but others live in unhappy homes where there is little care and love—'

The housekeeper entered the study without knocking.

'Has that boy gone, Father?' she asked bluntly.

'Yes,' replied the priest.

'He shouldn't be coming round here at this time of night,' she said.

'Was there something you wanted, Miss Evans?' asked the priest.

'Next time he comes, shall I tell him you're busy? You have quite enough to do without children calling round at all hours.'

'No, Miss Evans,' he said. 'If the child calls again I will see him. Now, was there something else?'

'There's a man at the door now. He wants to see you. I said that you have mass in an hour, but he won't take no for an answer.'

'You had better show him in,' said the priest.

It was the young man whom Father McKenzie had seen in church some weeks before.

'I'm sorry to disturb you, Father,' he began.

'It's Mark, isn't it?'

'That's right. I won't take up much of your time. I know that you have to get ready for mass, but I just wanted to speak to you.'

'Sit down,' said the priest.

'No, I'm not staying long. I wanted to see you to tell you that I took your advice. I thought about what you said to me and I talked to my mother. It was a long, hard talk but we seem to have sorted things out. You were right—when I had time to think about things and let it sink in, I sort of came to terms with it. I think I understand now why they never told me the truth. I still don't agree with what she and my father did. I might have tried to find my other mother. I still might. They were worried deep down that I would feel differently about them. I never would have. It's silly what people think, isn't it?'

'It is,' said the priest.

'And you know you asked me if I wondered why my mother chose this time to tell me?'

'Yes?'

'Well, I asked her. She's ill, Father. She's very ill. I don't think she's got a lot more time.'

'I see.'

'I guess she wanted to clear things up before . . . well, before she died. You were right, she does need me more than ever now. As I said, perhaps later I'll try and find my other mother.'

Father McKenzie would have liked to tell the young man about Miss Rigby, who had given her child up for adoption, and what she was feeling. But he knew he could not.

'I just wanted you to know, Father,' said the young man, 'that talking to me as you did, listening to what I had to say and what I felt, was really helpful. It helped me sort things out in my head. I was feeling so low that day. I'll go now, but I just wanted you to know that.' He shook the priest's hand.

'Keep in touch, Mark,' said the priest, 'and if you do try to find your other mother, I wish you luck. I will pray for you.'

Chapter Nine

'There's a woman in the church, Father,' said the housekeeper. 'She wants to see you. I think it's that boy's mother.'

Father McKenzie rose slowly from his desk. The pain in his side was there all the time now. He bit his bottom lip and steadied himself on the table.

'Are you all right, Father?' she asked.

'Yes, thank you, Miss Evans,' he said. 'Just a bit of a twinge.'

'I get them all the time these days,' she told him. 'It's a sign of old age.'

'Yes, indeed,' said the priest.

In the church porch stood a large, quite attractive young woman with dyed blonde hair. She had heavily made-up eyes and looked like a panda.

'Mrs Brown?' said the priest.

She was clearly startled by the mention of her name.

'Yes, that's right,' she said, 'and how would you know that?'

'You're Matthew's mother?'

'I am, yes.'

'I think your son might have mentioned it,' the priest told her. 'Would you like to come into the church and sit down?'

'No thanks, vicar. Churches give me the creeps. I'm all right out here.'

'What can I do for you?' asked Father McKenzie.

'It's about our Matty. He's been coming here, hasn't he?'

'He has, yes.'

'I couldn't get it out of him at first. I thought he was up to no good, going out and not telling me where. When he came in the other night, I asked him where he'd been, but he wouldn't say. I wouldn't know he came here now if that nosy old cow in the post office hadn't told me. She says she's heard that he's always round the church.'

'He likes to come here,' said the priest.

'It's not natural, a lad of his age spending his time in an old church,' said the woman. 'He should be playing football with his mates.'

'Perhaps so,' said the priest, 'but I don't think he's got any friends.'

'Well, whose fault it that?' she asked. 'Anyway, I hope he's been no trouble. He's always running off. I don't know why he keeps on bothering you, vicar.'

'He's no bother,' said Father McKenzie. 'As I said, he likes coming into the church.'

The woman gave a grunt. 'I don't know why. I can't remember the last time I set foot in a church. Mind if I smoke?'

Before he could answer, she dug into a large black shiny plastic handbag and produced a packet of cigarettes.

'Want one?' she asked.

'Thank you, no,' said the priest.

She lit a cigarette and took a deep in-drawing breath before noisily blowing out a cloud of smoke. She picked a small piece of tobacco from the tip of her tongue. 'Has he been saying things about me, vicar?' she asked.

'Saying things?'

'You know, what it's like at home, that sort of thing.'

'He's not said very much,' the priest told her.

'It's just that I don't want Social Services around again, poking their bleeding noses into my affairs. I've already had them round after some nosy busybody said I was neglecting him. I bet it was that old cow at the post office. You've not been on to Social Services, have you, vicar?'

'No, I haven't.'

'Well, I'm glad about that. I had this woman round. She didn't say I was a bad mother in so many words, but I knew what she was thinking. I could see it in her eyes. She asked Matty all these questions, about why he was missing school, and what it was like at home, and all about the trouble he got into down at the flats.'

'He didn't mention that,' said the priest.

'Lighting fires, he was, with some bigger lads. I reckon they put him up to it. I had to collect him from the police station.'

'He's not a very happy boy, Mrs Brown,' said the priest.

She laughed. 'Who is? Look, vicar, I know I'm not the world's best mother. I know I could do better by him, but bringing up a kid by yourself with not much money coming in is bloody hard. Thing is, I don't want them taking him away, putting him in a home, fostering him out. It happened to me when I was young. I know what it's like. Nobody gives a toss about you. I was passed like a parcel from one place to another. I had to learn to stand on my own two feet pretty quickly. In the first foster home I was in the woman took my doll off me and gave it to her little girl. All she wanted me for was to clean and skivvy for her.' She was quiet for a moment. 'I don't want Matty going in no home. I want him with me. I know I complain about him, and say things to him that I don't mean and he can be a right little bugger at times, but I'd really miss him.'

'Have you told him that, Mrs Brown?'

'What?'

'That you would miss him if he wasn't around.'

'I don't go in for that sort of thing, vicar.'

'Perhaps you should. Perhaps he needs to hear it. Maybe Matthew needs to know that you want him around. When you were fostered, didn't you wish that sometimes somebody might tell you that you were loved, that you were important, that you were liked and wanted?'

'I'm not good with words,' she said.

'You don't need to be good with words to tell him that you love him. He just wants some attention. Perhaps that's why he gets into trouble and stays out, to get attention.'

'How is it that vicars always make me feel guilty?' she asked, smiling for the first time.

'From what I gather, Mrs Brown,' said the priest, 'I don't think Matthew gets on very well with your boyfriend.'

'Craig?' She tapped ash on the floor and inhaled another mouthful of smoke. 'He can be a right bastard at times—pardon my French, vicar—I'd be the first to admit that, but I've had worse. I used to live with this bloke who knocked me about. Split my lip more than once. Then he up and took all my money, sold the television set and cleared off. Good riddance, I said. Craig's got a temper on him but he never hits me, and he hasn't laid a hand on Matty.'

'I think Matthew feels a bit left out,' the priest told her.

'He's a real handful at times, you know. He can be as nice as pie one minute, and then the next he starts playing me up. He looks all innocent when he wants to, but he can be a real little bugger. I know he don't like me going out and bringing men home and that, but I gets lonely. I mean, I need company like everyone else. As I said, it's hard bringing up a kid on your own.'

'I'm sure it is.'

'Have you any kids?' she asked.

'No,' said the priest, smiling.

'I sometimes wish I hadn't, and then at other times I think what would I do without him.'

'Mrs Brown,' said the priest, 'I think Matthew is a lonely little boy. He's really quite desperate for some attention.'

'Well, as I said, it's his own fault if he's no friends. He should be out playing football like other kids his age, but all he does is mope around the house getting under my feet, and then he takes off for hours at a time. I mean, what kid his age spends all his time in an old church? It's not natural.'

'Matthew is a bright little boy, Mrs Brown. He's sharp and interested in things. He asks questions, he wants to know—'

'Tell me about it,' she said, dropping the cigarette and stepping on it. 'Never stops asking questions. Drives Craig mad.' She thought for a moment. 'You know, you're the first one to tell me he's bright, vicar. Teachers at his school are always on to me about how thick he is, and about his bad behaviour, answering them back, getting into trouble, not doing his work.'

'Well, he behaves himself when he's here,' said the priest, 'and I really don't mind him coming to the church. He's no trouble.'

'What about your wife? Does she not mind some kid hanging around?'

'I'm not married.'

'Who was the woman who I spoke to, then?'

'That was Miss Evans, my housekeeper.'

'Oh, I see.' Father McKenzie noted a trace of suspicion in the dark eyes. He guessed what she must be thinking. 'So what's your interest in him then?' she asked.

'My interest,' repeated the priest. 'I suppose I try to help people, listen to their worries, try to give them some advice.'

'Well, I hope you won't take this the wrong way, but I don't think it's a good idea Matty hanging around here all the time.'

'The church is always open, Mrs Brown,' said the priest. 'The doors are never shut to anyone. If you wish, however, I will tell Matthew when he calls in again that you would prefer him not to come back. You are his mother and you are the one he should listen to.'

The woman thought for a moment and looked the priest straight in the eyes. She saw something in them that made her feel strangely calm and comforted, something she could not explain, something she had never felt before.

'No, don't do that, vicar,' she said. 'I don't suppose it does any harm, does it, and it keeps him off the streets.'

Chapter Ten

'How are you feeling, Father?' Mr O'Neill, the cancer specialist, looked over the rims of his glasses.

'Not too bad,' the priest told him, trying to sound cheerful.

'You don't look too good.'

'No,' admitted the priest, 'but that was to be expected.'

'You missed your last two appointments at the hospital.'

'I've been busy,' the priest told him.

'Too busy to come in and see how things are?'

'I think we both know how things are.'

'And have you been taking the medication?'

'The tablets made me feel worse.'

'Dear me, Father McKenzie, what are we going to do with you? I really think you ought to come in and let

96

me have a proper look at you.'

'It's thoughtful of you to ask, Mr O'Neill,' said the priest, 'and I am very grateful for your interest, but I think you have done all you can for me. The radiotherapy you suggested and the coloured pills will only delay things. To be honest, they will make me feel a whole lot worse. I would like to make the best of the time I have left.'

'I see,' said the specialist. 'Well, of course, that is your choice. Have you thought about when you get too ill to go on?'

'Oh yes,' the priest told him. 'That's all been sorted out. I've arranged to go into St Catherine's Hospice. It's run by a very nice order of nuns, and being a priest I reckon I'll get the five-star treatment.'

'You're a remarkable man, Father McKenzie,' said the doctor. 'A remarkable man. You are facing things with great courage.'

'I don't feel very brave, just rather

weary. You know, to live for a long time, Mr O'Neill, is not in itself an achievement. It's really about what you do with your life. I think in my small way I may have made a small difference in people's lives.'

ˣ 'I am sure you have. I have to tell you, Father, that you have made a difference in mine. I'm not a person who believes in an afterlife. I think that when we are dead that is the end. I wish I could believe as you do, that I had your faith. I am sure it has helped you through all this.'

'It has,' agreed the priest. He smiled.

'Is there anything I can do?' asked the specialist.

'Nothing,' said the priest.

Mr O'Neill got up and held out his hand. 'Well, you know where I am, Father McKenzie. I'll call in to the hospice when you are settled there.' He shook the priest's hand.

Father McKenzie left the warmth of the hospital and walked out into the bright cold December sunlight. It was a chilly day and he wished he had put on his coat. He headed for the park, as he usually did after the hospital visit, to sit and think things over for a while before returning to the church. He walked past the children's playground and sat well away from it, on a bench which faced the paddling pool. There would be no children paddling at this time of year, he thought. He eased himself down on to the park bench and bowed his head in prayer.

'Are you ill?'

It was the boy, standing by his side.

'Matthew,' said the priest, looking up. 'Where did you come from?'

'I was on the swings.' He pointed to the children's playground. 'I saw you come out of the hospital. You're ill, aren't you?'

'I'm not so good at the moment,' the priest said. The boy sat next to him.

'I thought you were ill. I could tell

when I last came into the church. You were breathing funny and holding your side.'

'You're a sharp young man,' said the priest. 'You never miss a trick.'

'Will you get better?' asked the boy.

'No, I don't think I will.'

'Are you dying?'

Children, thought the priest, were nothing if not blunt. 'Yes, Matthew, I am,' he said quietly.

'I didn't know,' said the boy.

'No one knows, and I think we should keep it that way for the time being.' The priest could picture the letter to the bishop propped up on his desk, unposted. He should have sent it long ago. I'll send it soon, he thought.

'Are you scared?' asked the boy.

'No, I don't think I am,' said the priest.

'I'd be scared.'

'You're only young,' he told him, giving a small smile. 'Young people don't think about dying. They think they will live for ever. I know I did when I was your age.'

'I do sometimes,' said the boy. 'Think about dying.'

'You shouldn't, Matthew. You have your whole life ahead of you, lots to look forward to. Everything for you should be new and exciting. You must make the most of it.'

'Craig's gone,' said the boy.

'Ah,' sighed the priest. 'I thought you looked more cheerful.'

'My mam kicked him out. It was after my mam had been to see you. It was something you said to her. She didn't shout at me when I got in. She just talked to me about things, said things would get better. When Craig came in later he was drunk and started shouting at me and my mam shouted at him. They had a big row. She told him to piss off.' The priest raised an eyebrow. 'Sorry,' said the boy, 'to leave, I mean.'

'And have things been better?'

asked the priest.

'Yeah, they have.'

'I'm pleased.'

'What did you say to her?' asked the boy.

'Not a lot,' said the priest.

'Thanks, anyway,' he said. 'For what you said to her.'

'And have you read some of the book I gave you?' asked the priest.

'I've looked at the pictures,' the boy told him.

'Try reading the stories,' said the priest. 'They are very good.'

They sat there in silence for a while, the boy close to the priest.

The park-keeper appeared silently, unannounced, hard-faced.

'Do you know this man?' he asked the boy.

'What's it to you?' asked Matthew.

'Don't you be cheeky!' snapped the park-keeper. 'I asked if you know him.'

'Yeah, I know him.'

'The boy comes to my church,' the

priest said quietly.

'You're a vicar?' the man asked.

'A priest.'

'I see.'

'Why don't you go and pick some litter up, grandad,' said the boy, 'and stop bothering us?'

'Why don't you watch your mouth?' replied the park-keeper.

'Don't be rude, Matthew,' said Father McKenzie.

'I reckon it's this little devil who's been writing on the walls near the kiddies' paddling pool and throwing stones at the ducks,' the park-keeper told him.

'I don't think so,' said the priest. 'He's been with me.'

'Yes, well, I'm keeping my eyes open,' the park-keeper said. He pulled a face and strode off.

'He's always on at me, that bloke. Tells me to get off the swings, walk on the path, keep off the flowers.'

'He has a job to do.'

'Parks are supposed to be for kids

as well as adults,' said the boy. 'He should want people to come into the park, not keep them away. He's watching us now. I can see him.'

'I'm pleased to hear things are better at home,' said the priest, changing the subject.

'What did you say to my mam?'

'Just that she might like to spend a bit more time with you, listen to you a little more. She told me she likes having you around, that she would be lonely without you, that she loves you.'

'She never said that,' said the boy.

'Well, near enough,' said the priest, smiling. 'She really does care for you, you know. Now you run off home and try to be a good boy. Tomorrow, if you come and see me, you can give me a hand getting the church ready for Christmas.' It will be a Christmas, thought the priest, that I might never see.

'OK,' said the boy. 'It wasn't me who threw stones at the ducks, you know.'

'I'm glad to hear it.'

The boy gave a wide grin. 'But I did write things on the walls near the paddling pool.'

Chapter Eleven

'I've put the Christmas things and the crib in the porch, Father McKenzie,' said the housekeeper.

'Thank you,' said the priest.

'Do you want some help putting them up?' she asked.

'I think I have a little helper here, Miss Evans,' he said. Then, turning to the boy, he asked, 'You're going to help me put up the crib for Christmas, aren't you, Matthew?'

'Yeah.'

'I think we can manage, thank you, Miss Evans,' said the priest. His voice was kindly.

'Very well, Father,' she said. Her heels clicked on the hard floor as she walked quickly away.

'What's a crib?' asked the boy.

'Surely you've seen a crib, Matthew?'

'Don't think so.'

'It's a model of Christ's nativity, His birth. There's a stable with hay, and figures of the baby Jesus, Mary, His mother, Joseph, the wise men, shepherds and angels and the animals.'

'Oh, yeah, I've seen one in the big shopping centre in town.'

The crib that the priest carried from the porch was a large but very sorry-looking item, made of dull strips of wood stuck together. He set it up below the Lady Altar. In a cardboard box were scraps of faded hay and huge figures which looked old and worn. The white paint had flaked off the baby Jesus, giving Him an unhealthy grey appearance. Joseph had lost a couple of fingers and the angels had lost their haloes. The three kings looked like down-and-outs, and the ox and the ass were chipped. Someone had tried to brighten up the Virgin Mary by repainting her with long yellow hair, bright red lips, crimson cheeks and an electric blue cape. She had a strange smile on her face. As he looked at her, Father McKenzie thought that the word 'virgin' was an unlikely word to describe her.

'It's a bit past its sell-by date,' said the priest.

The boy held up the figure of Mary. 'She looks like one of them women what hang about at the corner of our street,' said Matthew.

'Yes, she is a little bright, isn't she?' said the priest.

The boy looked at the figure of Joseph. 'This one looks as if he's lost a fight. It's Joseph, isn't it? He was a carpet fitter, wasn't he?'

'Carpenter,' said the priest, smiling.

'Yeah, I know,' said the boy, with a playful look in his eyes, 'I was being funny.'

'My father was called Joseph,' said the priest, recalling for a moment the last time he had seen him, and how he had changed, the grey lined face above the whiteness of the sheet, the thin bony hands. 'You're a good son,' he had said. 'I never said it to you but I am so proud of you.' There was a sort of pleading in the eyes. 'You know that, don't you?'

'Is this the incense?' asked the boy, picking up a small brown pot.

'It is,' said the priest. 'The wise men brought the baby gifts of gold, myrrh and frankincense.'

'I didn't get anything last Christmas,' said the boy. 'My mam was out at the pub most of the time. She said Father Christmas had run out of presents when he got to our house. I stopped believing in Father Christmas when I was a little kid. I watched telly all day.'

'Well, maybe you'll get something this year,' said the priest.

'Yes, my mam says she's getting me something special.'

'And how have things been at home?' asked the priest.

'Better.'

'That's good.'

'They've got a much nicer crib in the shopping centre in town,' the boy told Father McKenzie. 'This one's really tatty.'

'I always meant to replace the figures,' said the priest, 'but I never got around to it. And, you know, I have a certain liking for them. They're familiar. They were here when I came to this church many years ago.'

'The stable's crap as well,' said the boy. 'Sorry, I mean not very good.'

'But that's what it probably would have looked like, Matthew,' the priest told him. 'Baby Jesus was born in a stable, a cattle shed, and He only had a manger for a bed. It wouldn't have been nice and clean and bright like the crib in the shopping centre. The stable baby Jesus was born in would have been full of rather smelly animals and dirty hay. There was no room in the inn, you see, so Mary and Joseph had to stay in the stable and it didn't have lovely furniture and carpets and central heating. Mary had to have her baby in a cold, dark barn.'

'In a barn?'

'That's right. He had no nice new clothes, no toys and no cot. He came into the world with nothing. He was one of the poor and mean and lowly.'

Mathew shook his head slowly and said quietly but with feeling, 'Poor little bugger.'

'Matthew!' said the priest.

'Sorry,' said the boy.

The priest put his arm around the boy's shoulder and they stood together for a moment looking at the Christmas scene.

'Well, I think we've done enough for today, Matthew,' said the priest.

Neither of them saw the two figures who had walked quietly down the centre aisle and now stood behind them.

'Father McKenzie?'

The priest turned to face a young

man and a woman. He smiled. 'I didn't hear you come in,' said the priest.

'It is Father McKenzie?' asked the man again.

'It is,' he replied. 'I thought it was tomorrow that you young people were coming to see me.'

'Tomorrow?' said the man. 'You were expecting us?'

'I take it that you are John and Patricia, here to see me about the wedding arrangements.'

'No, sir, we're not. We're police officers. I'm Sergeant Vaughan and this is Police Constable Townsend.' The man took a small black warrant card from his inside pocket to show the priest.

'You wish to see me?' asked Father McKenzie.

'If we might have a word with you, sir.'

'Yes, of course.'

'I thought you were coppers,' said Matthew. 'Soon as I saw you, I thought you were.'

'Might we have a word with you in private, sir?' asked the policeman.

'Yes, of course,' said the priest. 'You run along now, Matthew, and thank you for helping me.'

'See you again,' said the boy, walking off. 'I'll try and get some fresh hay for the crib.'

'Would you like to come through to the house?' the priest asked the police officers.

'There's really no need for that, sir,' said the policeman. 'We won't take up too much of your time. It's just a routine visit.'

'Well, Sergeant Vaughan, what can I do for you?'

'Was that the young man who visits the church?' asked the sergeant.

'It is. He's not in any trouble, is he?'

'No, sir, he's not in any trouble.'

'That's good to hear,' said the priest. 'I thought for a moment he might be.'

'We have had a complaint,' said the policeman. 'Well, not really a complaint, more a piece of information that you spend a great deal of time in the park, near the playground, watching the children.'

'I beg your pardon?' asked Father McKenzie. His heart began to thump in his chest and he felt hot.

'We have been informed that you spend quite a lot of your time in the park watching the children,' repeated the policeman.

'Is that illegal?' asked the priest.

'Not illegal,' said the woman police officer, speaking for the first time, 'but unwise.'

'I do spend time in the park and it is true I enjoy watching the children play. Is there something wrong in that? How is it unwise?'

'It's just that we have to be very careful these days where young children are concerned,' said the policeman.

'Of course,' said the priest, 'I know

that.'

✗'People might get the wrong idea,' said the woman. 'An older single man spending his time watching children in the park.'

'The wrong idea?' repeated the priest.

'Yes, sir, the wrong idea. Then there's the boy. I believe he spends a lot of time here?'

'You seem to have a very good informant.'

'Actually it was another person who contacted us. She was concerned.'

'Sergeant Vaughan,' said Father McKenzie, finding it hard to get his breath, 'are you suggesting . . .'

✗'I'm not suggesting anything, sir,' said the policeman. 'What I am saying to you is that we have had passed on to us pieces of information about you. We have to follow things up. We've looked into it, spoken to people, and I think it would be a good idea if you didn't continue going to the park to watch the children.'

'I also think it would be sensible not to encourage the boy to visit the church,' added the policewoman.

'You have to be very careful these days when it comes to children,' said the sergeant.

'It's for your own good,' added the woman.

'Have you spoken to Matthew?' asked the priest.

'There is no need for that.'

'Perhaps you should have a word with him,' said the priest sharply, 'and get the right idea about why he comes here.'

'Let me be frank with you, Father McKenzie. The papers are full of people who have taken advantage of children, some of them, I am sad to say, people in your profession. You must see that it is rather ill-advised for an elderly man to spend his time watching young children and encouraging them to visit him. I'm

116

not for one moment saying that anything is happening here, but you have to be very careful. I suggest you change what happens in your church and keep away from the children.'

'It's for your own good,' added the policewoman again.

Chapter Twelve

Father McKenzie awoke with the pain in his side again. It had got worse over the last few days, so much worse that he decided he must face the fact that his time was running out. He had arranged to go into the hospice for the last few weeks. The letter had been posted to the bishop. Now he had to tell Miss Evans.

She was very pleasant that morning. 'You've not eaten your breakfast again, Father,' she said, fussing around him. 'You'll waste away.'

'I'm really not that hungry, thank you, Miss Evans,' said the priest.

'You ought to eat something.'

'Thank you, no.'

'You don't look all that well.'

'I'm just a bit under the weather,' he told her. This was now the time, he thought, to break the news to her.

'I don't suppose that boy will be coming back,' she said.

'Why do you suppose that?' asked the priest.

'No reason, Father,' she said, and changed the subject. 'I heard in the post office yesterday that Miss Rigby's passed on,' she said.

'Oh, I'm sorry,' said the priest. He sighed. 'She was a good woman.'

'She was a queer old stick and no mistake,' said the housekeeper, 'but she never missed mass, I'll give her that. First through the door, she was, always wearing that old hat and coat. The woman in the post office used to say she came in to collect her pension, never said a word, never posted a letter, and always wore that bright red lipstick and painted-on eyebrows. She said she kept her face in a jar by the door, back home in that run-down flat of hers.'

'I shall miss her,' said the priest. Poor Miss Rigby did not have much of a life, he thought. She was a sad and lonely woman, living alone in her dark, cramped little flat, spending her days thinking of a son she would never see. 'Do you know who is dealing with the funeral arrangements?' he asked. 'I don't believe she has any family. Perhaps you might ask your informants in the post office.'

'My informants?' repeated the housekeeper.

'They do appear to know everything that goes on,' said the priest.

'I'll do that, Father,' said the housekeeper. Her face had turned pink when he had mentioned the word 'informants'. 'Well, I had better get on,' she said.

'Would you mind sitting down a moment, Miss Evans,' said Father McKenzie. 'I would like to have a word with you.'

'I'm just about to put a rice pudding in the oven, Father,' she told him.

'It will wait. This is important. Do sit down. It won't take a minute. I have something I wish to speak to you about.'

The housekeeper refused to meet his gaze and stared down at the worn carpet. 'Before you start, Father,' she said, 'I want you to know that I never meant it to go this far. I never thought that Mrs Leary and those in the post office would contact the police.'

'Pardon?' asked the priest.

'Those two people who were talking to you in the church. They were police officers, weren't they?'

'Yes, they were,' said the priest.

'They were here about the boy.'

'Yes, they were here about Matthew, among other things.'

'I just didn't want things to get out of hand,' the housekeeper told him. 'I should never have mentioned it to Mrs Leary and Mrs Wilson in the first place, but we got talking about that boy always hanging about the church. I'd forgotten I'd said anything to her, it was that long ago. Then I was in the post office last week and Mrs Leary was telling the postmistress about him. I had mentioned it to her a while back, in passing. You know I was not keen on him coming here. That Mrs Leary has a tongue on her that could clip tin. Then Mrs Wilson said she'd seen you a few times with the boy and was saying that in her opinion it wasn't right—an old priest and a young boy spending all that time together. She thought something might be going on. Of course, they stopped talking when I got to the counter and they looked at me in a funny way as if I was involved in something. I was shocked and upset to hear them gossiping like that. She's like the jungle telegraph, that woman in the post office. Gossip like that could spread like wildfire. It made you sound as if you were up to no good, Father, as if you had some hidden motive for letting the boy visit you. I tried to tell them, I did, but . . .'

'Let me stop you, Miss Evans,' said the priest quietly.

The housekeeper carried on talking. 'People are all too ready, Father, at putting two and two together and getting five. I did say to you that I thought it would lead to no good. You're just too trusting, Father. The world is different now from what it was when we were young. You can't so much as look at a child without somebody thinking you're up to something. Then the boy's mother came round and I could see there would be trouble. I'm so sorry, Father. I should never have opened my mouth. I really didn't want it to go this far.'

'Well, Miss Evans,' said the priest, 'the police, as you said, have had a word with me, and I am a little upset about it, but that is not what I wanted to talk to you about. It was to tell you that next week I shall be leaving.'

'Leaving!' cried the housekeeper.

'That's right. I shall be leaving St Jude's next week.'

'Is it the bishop who's moving you?' asked the housekeeper. Her words were quick and anxious. 'Has he got word of the police calling to see you? I'm not the reason for you being moved, am I? You are not leaving because of me?'

'No, no, nothing of the sort,' the priest told her.

'Oh, well, that's a relief. But why are you going, Father? Where are you going?'

'I'm going into hospital,' the priest told her.

'Are you ill?'

'Yes, I am.'

'Is it serious?'

'I'm afraid it is,' said the priest. 'I have a terminal illness and I shall be going into St Catherine's Hospice.'

'Dear God,' said the housekeeper, putting her hand to her throat. 'I didn't know.'

'I have kept things pretty much to myself,' said the priest. 'I wanted to carry on as long as I was able.' The housekeeper started to cry. 'Please don't upset yourself, Miss Evans. I am quite prepared and I am not at all afraid. We all have to meet our maker one day.'

'I feel terrible, Father, I really do,' said the housekeeper. 'You being so ill all the time, and then me going on about the boy.'

'It's all water under the bridge now,' said the priest. 'I guess I won't see the young man again. I have written to the bishop to tell him, and I have asked him if you can stay on to help the new priest settle in. You have been a very good housekeeper and I'm sure the new priest will want you to remain.'

'Oh, Father McKenzie,' said the housekeeper, sniffing into her handkerchief. 'I'm so sorry.'

The priest went over and rested a

125

hand on her shoulder. 'And now perhaps you might like to put that rice pudding in the oven. Do you know, I think I could eat some.'

Chapter Thirteen

The following morning Father McKenzie had a visitor. He was a small, portly man with a round red face, large hands and fluffy little tufts of silver hair growing above his large ears. He wore a loud suit and a mustard-coloured waistcoat with a silver watch chain. He reminded the priest of a toby jug.

'I'm Mr Crisp,' he said, 'of Morton, Ridley and Crisp, solicitors.'

The priest's heart jumped. Now what, he thought.

'I'm not in any trouble, am I, Mr Crisp?' he asked.

'Dear me, no,' replied the solicitor.

'Well, what can I do for you?'

'May I take a seat?' the visitor asked, placing himself squarely on the sofa without waiting for a reply. 'I am here representing a client.'

'I see,' said the priest.

'Miss Eleanor Mary Rigby. I believe she was a parishioner here at St Jude's?'

'That's right.'

'You may or may not be aware that she died recently.'

'Yes,' said the priest. 'My housekeeper told me yesterday. I was wondering about the arrangements for the funeral. I would like to celebrate a requiem mass for her.'

'That's one of the reasons for my visit, Father McKenzie,' Mr Crisp told him. 'I would like to fix the date for the funeral and sort out the details for the burial. As the executor of Miss Rigby, I am acting on the instructions contained in her will. She wanted you to say the mass and bury her. I was thinking of next Thursday, if that is convenient.'

'That would be fine,' said the priest.

'I would have liked to have been here myself,' he said, 'but it is such a busy time of year and there is so much to do.'

'I understand,' said the priest.

'Miss Rigby wished to be buried in the churchyard if that can be arranged.'

'Yes, I am sure it can,' said the priest. 'I'll make the arrangements. Miss Rigby will be missed. She was a simple, kindly soul.'

'And a very rich one,' added the solicitor.

'I beg your pardon?'

'She left a large estate in property and shares. Of course, her father, Thomas Rigby, was a man of some wealth.'

'I never knew.'

'Oh yes,' said the solicitor, leaning back on the sofa. 'He was in textiles. You must have heard of Rigby Woollens and Worsteds?'

'I had no idea that she was his daughter,' said the priest.

'It was the biggest mill in the area at one time. Miss Rigby nursed her father for many years after his stroke. She was a saintly soul. She seemed like a little mouse, at her father's beck and call all the time. Thomas Rigby was, how shall I put it, a difficult man, and treated his daughter, as indeed he did everyone, as if she were a servant. In actual fact she was employed by him in his office when she was younger. No, he was not an easy man. After his death Miss Rigby, who was quite a beauty in her time, became something of a recluse, only coming out to visit your church, which I know gave her great peace of mind. She lived a simple life, although her father left her enough money to live very comfortably, very comfortably indeed.'

'I had no idea,' said the priest.

Mr Crisp placed his hands over his large stomach. 'And you, Father McKenzie, are the only person named in her will.'

'I'm what?'

'You are her sole heir.'

The priest was stunned. 'She left *me* her money?' he asked.

'Yes, indeed,' said the solicitor. 'All of it. At a rough estimate the estate, after the payment of death duties and fees, amounts to more than three million pounds.'

'Good gracious!' cried the priest. 'And she left it all to the Church?'

'No, no, Father, not to the Church, to you. She was very particular about it. It was written into her will that she wanted everything to go to you personally, to do with as you wish. She said in her will that you were the only person in her life who had time for her and who listened to her.' He pulled a piece of paper from his pocket. 'Perhaps you might like to hear what she wrote.' He coughed. He read. ' "Father McKenzie has done more for me than anyone else in this sad and lonely world. He made me feel my own goodness, and passed over all the many foolish and weak things everyone else found

131

in me. He drew out into the light all the good things only he could find in me and all this he did with his kind words. He is a very special man and, if there are such things as saints, he is one." '

'I don't know what to say,' said the priest.

'I have dealt with many wills in my time, Father McKenzie,' said Mr Crisp, 'but I have never read anything like this. You must be, as Miss Rigby says, a special sort of person.'

The housekeeper knocked and entered.

'I was wondering if your visitor would like a cup of tea?' she asked.

'No, thank you, dear lady,' said Mr Crisp. 'I must be off.' He rose from the sofa. 'Well, goodbye, Father McKenzie. I will be in touch with further details of the funeral and the various papers for you to sign.'

The housekeeper looked at the priest, hoping he might share the information with her, but he merely said, 'Please show Mr Crisp out, will you, Miss Evans?' He was lost for words.

*   *   *

It was a cold, rain-blackened December day when Miss Rigby was buried. An icy wind rattled the branches high in the trees, and rooks cawed overhead. Father McKenzie stood alone as the plain wooden coffin was lowered into the ground. As he recited the prayers his breath rose like steam in the wintry air. No one had come to the requiem mass. No one stood with him at the graveside. Father McKenzie shook the dirt off his hands as he walked away from the grave, thinking about how many lonely people there were in the world.

Miss Evans, with a running cold, had stayed indoors in the warmth. She appeared at the study door later that morning, her eyes red-rimmed, to help Father McKenzie pack a few things to take with him to the hospice.

'There will, no doubt, be other things I will need,' the priest told her cheerfully. 'I can always send for those, if you wouldn't mind bringing them in.' He sounded as if he were going on holiday.

'Not at all, Father,' she said sadly.

'I had thought perhaps that I would be here for Christmas,' said the priest, taking down a small gold-framed print of the Virgin and Child from the wall, 'but that was not to be.'

'You will be missed, Father,' said the housekeeper unhappily.

'I hope so,' replied the priest.

'I'll miss you, Father,' she said, snuffling into her handkerchief.

'And I you, Miss Evans.'

She sat on the sofa and began to weep.

'Now come along, don't be

miserable. It's not the end of the world, as my mother used to say.' Of course, as soon as he had said it, he realized that for him it soon would be the end of the world. He changed the subject. 'It was quite a surprise,' he said, 'Miss Rigby having all that money.'

'I know,' sniffed the housekeeper. 'We were all surprised. To look at her you wouldn't think she had two pennies to rub together.'

'Indeed,' agreed the priest. 'I am sure she would have been pleased that it has been put to such good use.'

Later that day the bishop called to see Father McKenzie.

The two men, who had trained together in Maynooth, talked of old times.

'You know, Father Michael,' the bishop said, 'when we studied together, it was you who everyone thought would rise up the ranks in the Church.'

'I have never regretted becoming a parish priest. I was never cut out to be a bishop.'

'I sometimes wonder whether I am cut out to be a bishop. My district is getting further and further in debt, I'm afraid.'

'I should tell you, Bishop John,' said the priest, 'that I have been left a large amount of money in a parishioner's will. It was a Miss Rigby. Her father owned a large mill.'

'That was very kind of her,' said the bishop. 'I am sure it will be put to very good use.'

'It was left to me personally and not to the Church.'

'I see.'

'I am minded to use it to get the church decorated, repair the roof, and get rid of that stain in the Lady Chapel. I thought of giving the rest to help with the diocese debt.'

'That would be very generous, Father,' said the bishop.

'But then I thought it could be put to much better use.'

The bishop cradled his hands in his lap and waited.

'So I have decided to donate it to a children's charity,' said the priest. 'I want children who have very little in the world to benefit. It will go to the nuns in South America who care for the street children, those little scraps who live in the gutter, who have no family and who often disappear without trace.'

'You don't have to explain your decision to me, Father Michael,' said the Bishop. 'It is a very good plan. We will pray that God will help us clear the debt.'

Father McKenzie was surprised by the bishop's reply. 'You are not disappointed that I am not giving it to the Church?' he asked.

'No, Father, I think your Miss Rigby would have approved of where it is going.'

'So do I.'

The bishop smiled. 'And I will pray for you, Father Michael.'

Chapter Fourteen

Father McKenzie looked out of the lounge at the hospice over the long lawns, shimmering white with a carpet of thick snow. It was a strange, colourless world stroked by silence.

He watched the great flakes begin to settle and thought of his father and how he had hated the winter. The icy winds had raged around the lonely farmhouse. The snow had packed up in great mounds and piled into drifts which froze until the whole landscape had been changed into one vast ocean of rolling waves. He remembered his father's lonely figure, collie dog leaping at his heels, tramping through the thick snow in a field behind the barns in search of his sheep. He remembered well the grim expression on his face. His had been a hard life.

The priest's room at the hospice was full of cards and flowers. He had been amazed at the number of people who had visited, been in touch and sent letters.

'You are a very popular man, Father,' said the little nun who came in with yet another handful of mail. 'The Pope in Rome couldn't have had as many well-wishers.'

'Or better treatment, sister,' the priest added.

That morning he was sitting in the lounge watching the snow settle on the lawns when a young man came and sat by him.

'I thought it was you, Father,' he said.

'Mark,' said the priest.

'I'm sorry to see you here, Father,' he said. 'I'm here to see my mother.'

'I see,' said the priest.

'The doctors say she has only a few more days to live.' There were tears in his eyes. 'She's peaceful and in no pain.'

'I shall pray for her,' said the priest.

'I don't know your name,' said the young man.

'Father McKenzie.'

'Thank you, Father McKenzie, for listening. I was feeling pretty low when I came into your church that Saturday morning. As I told you, what you said to me really helped. I suppose you are told all the time how your words do help.'

'Will you try to trace your other mother?' asked the priest.

'I don't think so. What's the use? She probably started a new family after she gave me away and has forgotten about me by now. I don't think she would be all that pleased at me turning up on her doorstep and telling her I was her long-lost son.'

'Mark,' said the priest, 'let me tell you a story about Miss Eleanor Rigby.'

Back in his room the priest closed his eyes. Sometimes he had doubted if he did any good at all, that his advice was hollow or fell on stony ground, that he had little effect on people's lives. It was good to hear that he had made a difference.

'You have a little visitor,' said the nun.

Matthew stood by the door. His cheeks were apple red where he had scrubbed them. His hair was slicked down and his clothes were clean.

'Hello,' he said shyly.

'Hello, Matthew,' said the priest. 'My goodness, you do look smart.'

'I thought I'd better tidy myself up a bit to come and see you. They wouldn't let me in if I looked scruffy. My mam got me some new clothes.'

'Does your mother know that you are here?' asked the priest.

'Oh yeah,' he said. 'She got me a card to give you. I didn't bring it. It said "Get Better Soon!"'

'How did you manage to get past Sister Pauline?'

'I told her I was one of your altar

boys,' said the boy.

'Well, I'm pleased to see you. Come on in and sit over here by the window. Now how are things at home?'

'A lot better now that there's only my mam and me.'

'I'm glad.'

'She's been a lot better lately as well. I've been a lot better too. I'm getting on with her more and keeping out of trouble at school.'

'I'm very glad to hear it,' said the priest. 'You are a good lad, Matthew. Always remember that.'

'I wanted to see you,' said the boy. He was near to tears.

'How did you know I was here?' asked the priest.

'That old woman at the church, her who shouted at me, her who said she thought I was there to nick stuff, she told me.'

'Did she indeed?' said the priest.

'I stood outside the church and she came out. I thought she was going to tell me to go away, but she said you'd like to see me. She looked really upset.'

'Well, I'm pleased you came.'

'You know what,' said the boy, 'you're the only person who ever listened to me, the only one. My mam was always too busy and always going out, and the teachers made me feel like rubbish. You made me feel something inside when I talked to you. I can't explain it really. I just felt different with you. You made me feel that I wasn't useless or stupid.'

The priest's eyes began to fill with tears.

'I know they call you father,' said the boy, 'and that you don't have any kids of your own, which seems daft to me, but you ought to have had kids. You'd have been a really good dad.' He rubbed his eyes. 'I wish you had been mine.'

The boy rested his head on the priest's shoulder and began to cry softly.

'Matthew,' said the priest gently, closing his eyes. 'The name means "Gift of God", you know.'

Afterword

I grew up in the 1950s and 1960s, and like many at the time I loved the music of the Beatles. They changed the whole face of popular music. I would hum the tunes on the way to school. I knew all the words of 'Help!', 'A Hard Day's Night', 'Yesterday', 'Sergeant Pepper', 'Lucy in the Sky with Diamonds'. My favourite was 'Eleanor Rigby'. I don't know why this was my favourite, because it's really sad and all about these lonely people, unlike many of the Beatles' songs. I remember wondering what this woman Eleanor Rigby looked like and what sort of life she led. I tried to imagine the lonely old priest, Father McKenzie, darning his socks alone in the night-time. Well, perhaps they led lives like the characters in my story.